Diggy Mole's New Home

Written and Illustrated
by
Sue Camm

BRIMAX BOOKS • NEWMARKET • ENGLAND

Diggy is a mole. His coat is black and soft. He can dig in the ground with his strong front claws. He digs a long tunnel under the field by the river. This is where Diggy lives in a cosy home at the end of the tunnel. When the sun shines, Diggy Mole loves to sit and look at the river.

Today, Diggy wakes up with wet feet. When he jumps out of bed he lands in a puddle.
Splash!
Plop, plop, plop he goes along to his front door.
He looks outside.
"What can I do now?
I know what this is.
It is a flood!"
says Diggy.

The water from the river
has made a flood in his
field.
"Look what the flood has
done to my cosy home! This
is very bad. I must find
a new home to live in,"
says poor Diggy.
The water is not very deep.
He can make his way right
across the field
to the hedge.

Diggy must look for a new
home away from the water.
"A blackbird lives high up
in the hedge," says Diggy.
"It will not be wet there.
A bird's nest is just what
I need."
Diggy looks in the hedge
until he finds an empty
bird's nest. He climbs in.
"I will be dry
here," he says.

When night comes, Diggy
cannot sleep. The moon and
the stars are too bright.
"I do not want to live in
a home without a roof,"
says Diggy.
In the morning, he jumps
out of the bird's nest in
the hedge.
Diggy goes along the lane.
"What can I do?"
says poor Diggy.

Diggy begins to look for
a new home with a roof.
He meets a fat brown toad.
The toad says, "Come and
have a bite to eat with me."
He goes into Toad's home.
"If you want a home with
a roof, why not have
this flowerpot? I am
moving out today. You
can move in,"
says the toad.

When night comes, Diggy
cannot sleep. A flowerpot
home has cold walls.
The hole in the bottom
lets in the wind.
"I have never been so cold!"
says Diggy Mole.
"I do not want to live in
a cold home like this,"
says Diggy. Off he goes
down the lane
into a farmyard.

Diggy begins to look for
a new home that is warm.
He sees Mother Hen with
all her little chicks.
"Mother Hen takes care to
keep her chicks snug and
warm," says Diggy Mole.
"I can make a cosy home in
the henhouse. I can make
it with some straw." So then,
Diggy makes a
nice warm home.

When night comes, Diggy
cannot sleep. All the hens
begin to snore. All the
little chicks run about
after bedtime. They do not
want to go to bed.
Diggy is very very cross.
"I cannot stay here,"
says Diggy Mole.
In the morning, he goes
                out and across
                the cornfield.

Diggy begins to look for
a new home where no one
wakes him up at night.
He sees a big tree by the
side of the cornfield.
"This is just what I want,"
says Diggy Mole.
"I can make a home in the
roots of that tree. No one
will wake me up there."
Diggy begins to
make a new home.

When night comes, Diggy
cannot sleep. There is not
a sound. He is all alone.
Diggy feels afraid.
"I do not like to be alone,"
says Diggy. "I must go away
from here." In the morning,
he gets up. He goes away
from the tree. He goes along
a sandy bank.
He is very sad.
What can he do?

Diggy sees a little door
in the sandy bank. "Here
is a tunnel just like mine!"
he says. He looks inside.
Someone is coming along
the tunnel. It is someone
who has a soft black coat.
"Hello, I am Monty Mole,"
he says. "Come inside.
I live all by myself.
I am so glad to meet you."
Diggy goes into
the tunnel.

"The water made a flood in my home. I cannot find a new home," says poor Diggy. "A mole needs a tunnel and a cosy home to live in."

"It is great fun to share," says Monty. "You can have my spare room!"

"Hurray! Thank you, Monty!" says Diggy. "Now I have a new home and a new friend too!"

Say these words again

claws	bright
tunnel	toad
field	flowerpot
puddle	henhouse
splash	straw
flood	cornfield
warm	someone
hedge	myself
blackbird	sound
empty	coming